JOHN BURNINGHAM
HUSHABYE

ALFRED A. KNOPF
New York

For Madeleine

THIS IS A BORZOI BOOK PUBLISHED BY ALFRED A. KNOPF

Copyright © 2000 by John Burningham

All right reserved under International and Pan-American Copyright Conventions. Published in the United States of America by Alfred A. Knopf, a division of Random House, Inc., New York, and simultaneously in Canada by Random House of Canada Limited, Toronto. Distributed by Random House, Inc., New York. Originally published as *Husherbye* in Great Britain in 2000 by Jonathan Cape, Random House UK Limited. KNOPF, BORZOI BOOKS, and the colophon are registered trademarks of Random House, Inc.

www.randomhouse.com/kids

Library of Congress Cataloging-in-Publication Data
Burningham, John.
Hushabye / John Burningham.—1st American ed.
p. cm.
Rev. ed. of: Husherbye.
Summary: A cat, three bears, a fish, a frog, a baby, and others look for a place to go to sleep at the end of the day.
ISBN 0-375-81414-0 (trade)—ISBN 0-375-91414-5 (lib. bdg.)
[1.Sleep—Fiction. 2. Stories in rhyme.] I. Burningham, John. Husherbye. II. Title
PZ8.3.B9529 Hu 2001
[E]—dc21
00-067801
Printed in Hong Kong
October 2001
10 9 8 7 6 5 4 3 2 1
First American Edition

There's a cat with a stroller.
She's had a hard day and
now needs a place for
her kittens to stay.

HUSHABYE

The baby's been sailing
a boat on the sea
and now needs to sleep.
HUSHABYE

There are three tired bears
who are climbing the stairs.
HUSHABYE

And a fish in the sea,
it is weary you see.
HUSHABYE

And the man in the moon,
he'll be sound asleep soon.
HUSHABYE

The goose flying high
was too long in the sky.
HUSHABYE

There's a frog who's been hopping all day in the heat. He's tired and he's dry. HUSHABYE

Now we are tired,
we need to lie down.
It's time to sleep for the night.

When morning comes,
we will wake up again.
Tomorrow will be a new day.

The cat's found a place
for her kittens to stay,
out of the wind and the snow.

The baby's asleep
in the boat that's afloat
and is rocking on watery waves.

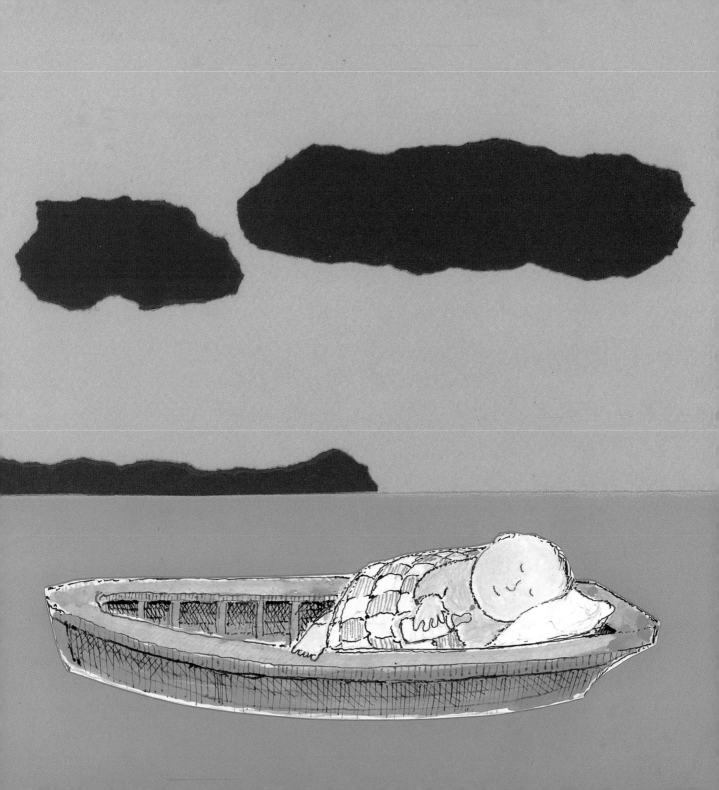

The three tired bears
who were climbing the stairs
are tucked up in their beds
until morn.

The fish in the deep
has fallen asleep
with his head on a pillow
of coral.

The man in the moon
will not wake until noon.
Then he'll shine up the
moon for tomorrow.

The goose is asleep now,
asleep in the chair,
and will fly off again
when it's light.

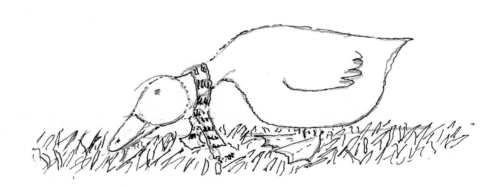

The frog did get wet and
now dreams in a net,
and he'll hop off once
more in the morn.

You are tucked up in bed.
Your toes are all warm.
You're out of the wind
and the rain.
Your head's on the pillow.
You'll soon be asleep.

HUSHABYE

HUSHABYE

HUSH

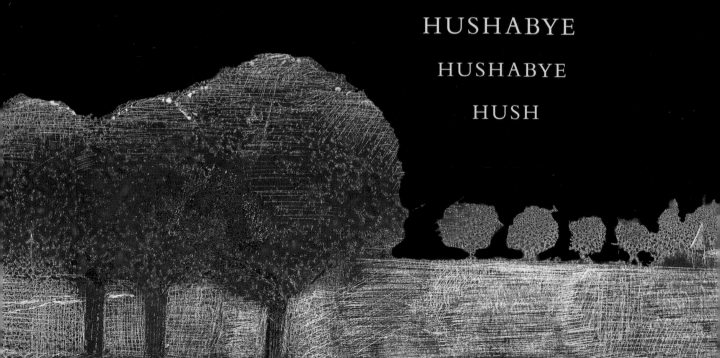